A FABLE OF
Liberty
Lost &
Found

Let us suppose a small number of persons
settled in some sequestered part of the earth,
unconnected with the rest, they will then represent
the first peopling of any country, or of the world.

THOMAS PAINE

A FABLE OF
Liberty Lost & Found

Inspired by Thomas Paine's
Common Sense

Judah Freed

Author of *Making Global Sense*

Hoku House

A FABLE OF LIBERTY LOST AND FOUND
Inspired by Thomas Paine's *Common Sense*

Author: Judah Freed
Published by Hoku House
Denver, Colorado, USA, Earth
HokuHouse.com | GlobalSense.com

Published in the United States of America; available worldwide.

Cloth Hardcover:	ISBN: 978-1-7373985-5-4
Trade Softcover	ISBN: 978-1-7373985-6-1
eBook:	ISBN: 978-1-7373985-9-2

Distributed to booksellers through Ingram and others.
The publisher at Hoku House handles special orders.

10 Percent of book royalties donated to literacy projects.

Library of Congress Control No. (Pending)

Cataloging-in-Publication Data:

Freed, Judah Ken 1950 —

A FABLE OF LIBERTY LOST AND FOUND

70 pages with an introduction, 10 sections and appendices.

1. Literary Fiction. 2. Fable. 3. Satire. 4. Dystopia. 5. Utopia.
6. Current Affairs/Politics. 7. Government. 8. Spirituality.

Dedications

For open democracy on our globe,
and for enlightenment in all forms.

For Thomas Paine, who showed up,
paid attention and spoke the truth.
May your writings uplift our world.
May your old soul smile in peace.

Here then is the origin and rise of government;
namely, a mode rendered necessary by the
inability of moral virtue to govern the world;
here too is the design and end of government,
viz. freedom and security.

THOMAS PAINE

Table of Contents

Society in every state is a blessing,
but government even in its best state is
but a necessary evil; in its worst state
an intolerable one.

THOMAS PAINE

Updating Paine's Parable

THOMAS PAINE opened *Common Sense* with a short parable about a remote community trying to govern itself. He used the fable to explain the different forms of government and how they arise. His pivotal essay persuaded colonial Americans to reject monarchy and establish the first modern republic. Paine's work changed the course of human events.

I've adapted his fable into a cautionary tale about what happens to government in any society that loses a natural spiritual sense of our oneness. Part I tells of an island society where free democracy rises and falls. Their misadventures are absurd and tragic.

Part II offers a more hopeful alternative ending, a playful vision of an enlightened democratic society. We need all the hope we can get these days.

I've expanded on Paine's first seven paragraphs in *Common Sense* (see original text in Appendices) to create ten sections, the length of a short story.

This fabricated fable began as the preamble and epilogue framing my nonfiction book, *Making Global Sense:* Grounded hope for democracy and the earth inspired by Thomas Paine's *Common Sense.*

The story holds its own solo, I realized, so here's my best effort to tell the tale well in one volume.

May you enjoy reading this small book as much as I've enjoyed creating it. When you finish, I hope you let it sit a bit. Insights may surface.

Judah Freed,
Denver

A FABLE OF

Liberty
Lost &
Found

Some writers have so confounded society with government, as to leave little or no distinction between them; whereas they are not only different, but have different origins. Society is produced by our wants, and government by our wickedness.

THOMAS PAINE

PART I

Liberty Lost

Government, like dress, is the badge
of lost innocence; the palaces of kings are
built on the ruins of the bowers of paradise.
For were the impulses of conscience clear,
uniform, and irresistibly obeyed, man [sic]
would need no other lawgiver.

THOMAS PAINE

Paradise Found

LET US IMAGINE a small group of brave humans who settle on a large, remote and unoccupied island paradise surrounded by a vast ocean.

Let us imagine all the settlers are enlightened, each attuned to the cosmos. Each has a global sense of universal oneness. Since all that exists is vibrating light, all are equal. Each feels inner peace and love for themselves, for other settlers, for the earth.

Among the immigrants is a young man named Kodesh. Like the others, he freely shares his true self in every moment. He treats other settlers and himself with respect, empathy, compassion, and humor.

Kodesh joins his fellow pioneers in building an inland hamlet. He joins other settlers in locating ley lines for building huts and community buildings.

Human beings are social animals innately unfit for total solitude. Kodesh cannot satisfy all desires by himself. He turns to others for help as others turn to him. Self-sufficiency is valued in any sane society, yet talents are most often noticed through service, such as divining where to dig a well in a drought.

Some settlers perish. Facing hardships together forges bonds of community among the people. They gather to plant a sapling tree in a field as a symbol of the settlement's faith and unity. They'd brought seeds from the old country of a species revered for mythic longevity. The tree will thrive as the people thrive. The community gathers around the tree to pray.

In their openly free society, rights and duties are shared fairly among all as natural equals. Aside from women bearing children, they have no gender roles. Each one's talents and interests guide what they do in the community. For instance, Kodesh harvests grain. His neighbor Shakti mills flour. People of any gender can do any task that's meaningful to them.

Kodesh now discovers that his friendship with Shakti has grown into love. Their hearts open to each other. They are in one another's dreams. Their souls unite when making love. They begin a family, happily raising two children with generous kindness.

Like others, Kodesh solves problems creatively. He welcomes advice and mediation from those with more wisdom and experience. He trusts conscience, intellect and intuition to reveal the best solutions. If any person is offended, honesty brings forgiveness. Kodesh and others agree everyone does the best they can do, given what they know at the time.

Sometimes the community gathers at the tree of unity. They decide issues together, like where to build a reservoir. Everybody talks until a decision is reached by consensus. Full community support of decisions is well worth their time. They learn patience.

The settlers live and thrive in joyful harmony because all the people rule themselves from within. Their respectful, graceful spirituality makes laws and government unnecessary. They share an unwritten, tacit "social contract" to govern their lives together with conscience and conscious self rule.

In this way, trusting mindfulness and personal sovereignty, the island community balances freedom and responsibility. Their peaceful, creative, utopian anarchy lasts as long as people behave themselves.

Thus necessity, like a gravitating power,
would soon form our newly arrived emigrants
into [a] society, the reciprocal blessings of which,
would supersede [vileness], and render the obligations
of law and government unnecessary while they
remained perfectly just to each other.

THOMAS PAINE

- 2 -

Democracy

BY THE FOURTH GENERATION on the island, the enlightenment of the first settlers has dwindled in their offspring. The spiritual tools for self rule are still taught to all of the children, yet the youngsters are distracted by the adventures of living in a growing community. The social mandate for mindful self rule fades in each new generation.

Initiation into spiritual sensitivity becomes a dry ritual with scant substance. People know oneness in their heads more than their hearts or guts.

With less spirituality to guide conduct, human frailties and vices surface. Envy and jealousy disrupt the peace. Some in the Kodesh family, for instance, resent how great-grandson Seth has prospered more than others in the clan.

The community faces cases of cheating, theft, rape, and murder. For safety, the women subtly cede power to the stronger men. Men compete intensely for the most desirable women. Distrust grows while the social fabric unravels at the edges.

The people decide to form a civil government to regulate society. They want a written social contract. So, they draft a "constitution." The paper spells out people's rights, liberties and duties in society.

The rule of law replaces self rule.

For major decisions, the community gathers at the Unity Tree. If a consensus can't be reached, they vote. They all vote. All votes are equal.

They thereby establish a *direct democracy*, also known as a real democracy, true democracy, pure democracy, and genuine democracy.

The community rules at first bear muted titles of "Guidelines," enforced mainly by social disdain — a cold shoulder. As more crimes occur, "Regulations" follow and then formal "Laws." As infractions happen more often, laws become more stern, consequences more severe. More Laws mean more "crime."

In extreme cases, such as a murder, the offender is banished. The person goes off alone to a secluded part of the island until they feel honest repentance.

When they meekly return, forgiveness welcomes them home, help them reenter society.

In this way, the people create a government to balance freedom and responsibility. Since they lack spirituality to govern themselves with full personal responsibility, they choose to be governed by the rule of law. Their democracy lasts as long as most people behave themselves.

They will mutually and naturally support each other,
and on this (not on the unmeaning name of king)
depends the strength of government,
and the happiness of the governed.

THOMAS PAINE

3

The Republic

THE ORIGINAL SETTLEMENT becomes a growing town. Other towns are soon built in more parts of the island. Agriculture expands and simple industries develop to meet island needs. Mining and smelting yields metals for tools and machines. Gems and minerals are traded for goods and services.

Before long, commerce replaces consciousness at the center of daily life. Society shifts.

The outer forms of spirituality matter more than actual awareness. Spiritual vestiges get codified into a formal religion. Priests preach that worldly riches are proof of God's approval and blessings.

In each town, a few families excel at building wealth. Strong men govern these clans. One such man is Peter Seth. He generously assists less-affluent neighbors and helps fund public works, like an island irrigation system with aqueducts.

In general, men do most of the managing and physical labor. Women's first job is motherhood. Mrs. Seth is lauded for bearing eight children. Women are honored for charitable works. A woman of valor is one who praises her husband in public.

Widening gaps in wealth incite more crime. The Great Council of all adults on the island enacts more laws. Town sheriffs refer cases to local judges, usually the elders. Population growth consumes territory once use for banishment, so punishment often is prison. Released offenders return home, but they're shunned until they prove themselves.

Meetings under the spreading Unity Tree grow too big to make decisions quickly. Many people now live too far away to attend every Council meeting, so they feel disenfranchised. Direct democracy seems like too much work. The people agree to leave the job of lawmaking to a few wise heads.

They amend their constitution, adopting a new form of government. They will elect representatives as proxies. Elected delegates will run island affairs for everyone. Decision-making power will shift from the people to their elected leaders.

Under this new social contract, the people form a representative democracy. To use the correct term, they form a *republic*. Abandoning direct democracy, people put their fate in the hands of those they elect. Delegates in the new congress share the concerns as those electing them. They vote the same as the whole island would vote, if all the people were present.

To avert corruption, publicly funded elections distribute tax funds equally to all the candidates and ballot measures. Public meetings educate all citizens. Each candidate and ballot measure receives equal opportunities to persuade voters. People prefer facts over opinions when assessing candidates and issues. Delegates and voters trust and respect one another. On this integrity depends the strength of any republic and the happiness of the governed.

In this way, people depend upon their leaders to help society balance freedom and responsibility. If the people elect wise leaders, such a republic lasts as long as most people behave themselves.

As they surmount the first difficulties of
emigration, which bound them together in a
common cause, they will begin to relax in their
duty and attachment to each other; and this
remissness [neglect] will point out the necessity
of establishing some form of government
to supply the defect of moral virtue.

THOMAS PAINE

4

Corruption

MORE GENERATIONS PASS. Government makes more choices that people once made for themselves. Government says when to harvest a field and where to grind the grain. Habits of mindfulness for social harmony are replaced by habits of obedience.

Spiritual consciousness is left to a few mystics and healers. They are tolerated, yet denied real social influence. Popular religion adapts to changing times. The clergy preaches that all people are born sinful. Salvation and a place in Heaven depend on obeying the Law. Priests proclaim defiant souls burn in Hell. Criminals go to an arid leeward purgatory territory, never to return. Good riddance of rubbish.

Over time, distinctive districts develop. Each district is run by a clique of wealthy families on grand estates. Each elite family has its own spokesman. The leading voice for the northern district is Albert Seth Cartman, a popular firebrand preacher.

District leaders complain local interests are not represented by islandwide delegates. Exerting their influence, the constitution is amended again.

Every district will elect its own representatives. District delegates should vote in congress the same as the majority in the district would vote if present. In reality, secret deals decide public policies.

The press exposes that congressman Al Cartman took bribes from northern district Landlop Mining. He was paid to pass a law granting immunity to water and soil polluters. Cartman apologizes, repays the bribe and resigns his seat in humiliation.

To fight corruption, people demand checks and balances in government. They alter the constitution for a separation of powers between three co-equal branches — legislative, executive and judicial.

Congress is now bicameral. The upper Senate represents the rich. The lower House represents the commoners. Each chamber of congress supposedly checks the other. In reality, the two bodies fight each other rather than serve all the people.

The executive branch gets a revamp.

The president is elected by a popular vote. This man (always a man) manages the agencies delivering civil services. Congress must ratify his budget, but the president can veto any law passed by congress, and his veto is difficult to override. The president further can issue "executive orders" that bypass congress, and the courts must enforce his orders.

A president can appoint judges for life through senate confirmation. The lower house gets no vote on judicial appointments. Only judges approved by the elites are allowed to decide legal disputes.

Al Cartman runs for president. Voters reject him. He denies any fault for his loss. He blames publicly funded elections for denying his "freedom of speech" to fight "lies" about his history. He claims elections cost taxpayers too much money, a big burden. Equal public funding for all candidates denies citizens the right to support only those they favor.

Cartman gathers allies urging campaign finance reform. All elections must be privately funded only by those who actually care about society. Funds may come from citizens, businesses, trade unions, and civic groups, but never from taxes, so taxes stay low for the common good. This time around, Cartman's con job is successful.

The constitution changes again. The elites gain more power than ever. Wealthy donors feel they own the politicians they help to elect. Politicians spend more time raising funds than passing laws. Still, their job *is* lawmaking, so they generate a vibrational field attracting problems to solve with more laws.

The people realize money buys the ballot box. They see their votes do not count or are not counted fairly. Many people stop voting. They feel powerless. They lose hope. Apathy spreads. Power shifts further to leaders. Entertainment and sports deflect people from noticing leaders' political sins.

Al Cartman, by now an influential media pundit, confounds voters by saying government itself is the problem. Let's cut the size and reach of government. Congress slashes public funds for education and the arts. Ignorance rises, as does poverty and its crimes. State security funding increases annually. People feel less secure than ever.

In this way, leaders deploy fraud to control the masses. They deprive the people of responsibility for their freedom. Such a corrupt republic lasts as long as enough willing people behave themselves.

5

Tyranny

THE CHASM BETWEEN the rich and poor widens in succeeding generations. People struggle to survive in this "republic." They rarely recall how they once lived in a real democracy. Memories of life without a government vanish into myth. People forget about ever practicing self rule. The children are taught the first settlers created a strong government.

Factories, shops and homes now fill the island — except for walled estates, the private lands used for raising food and the crowded purgatory territory. Agrochemical companies genetically modify crop seeds to require the pesticides and herbicides these companies sell for big profits. Farmers are forbidden to save seeds for replanting. They get annual loans to buy new seeds. Family farms are vanishing.

Feeding people should not require poisoning them, argues activist Kodesh Adoni Rafi. He starts a campaign to boycott "fake food" and eat organic. Mass media call him a "nature nut." He's mocked on a new network of networks, the "Internet."

A reactionary political party forms, led by Albert Cartman's grandson, Jason Cartman Bull. He blames all island woes on the nature nuts and "pagans" who cling to old ways and hate modern technology. Bull says pagans are "the enemy of the people."

With ample private funding, Jason Bull is elected president. Six months later, somebody bombs the Unity Tree. Bull blames the pagan "eco-terrorists" for attacking the "homeland." Congress then grants him emergency powers. People must temporarily give up a few liberties for "homeland security."

After a second bombing at the capitol building, terrified people do not object as Bull declares martial law. Bull equates dissent with treason. Troops guard street corners. Cameras everywhere see all. The state monitors calls and mail. Secret police at night detain dissenters without any trial, never to return.

The activist Rafi is arrested, tortured into a video confession and then found dead in his jail cell. Those questioning his death join the disappeared.

Bull proclaims he alone can fix island problems. He feeds on fanatical worship. Security fears isolate him and stymie his decision-making. His staff tells him only what feeds his ego. They filter out what does not serve his interests. He lives in an echo chamber. Inept and short-sighted policies prevail

Years of tyranny follow. A base of loyal followers swallows all state lies without thinking. Individuality is repressed. Conformity is rewarded. Free speech ends. Bull and his bullies get away with any dastardly deeds. Government loses all accountability.

The people forget the meaning of "freedom." They're unwitting slaves who cannot be free because they do not know they have a choice. To bemuse the masses, state mass media tout food, sex, drugs, and violent sports. People turn comfortably numb to the suffering in the world and in themselves. Without a binding spiritual feeling of community, the social contract finally breaks.

In this way, island society corrodes from within as people crave freedom not to behave themselves.

Absolute governments (tho' the disgrace of human nature) have this advantage with them, that they are simple; if the people suffer, they know the head from which their suffering springs.

THOMAS PAINE

6

Collapse

DECADES OF TYRANNY decay society. When aging Jason Bull nears death, his grip slips. Anxiety over life without a leader breeds chaos. Society disintegrates. People fear the end of the world is nigh.

Rafi's vengeful son, Gokillem, declares himself a savior and recruits a "people's army" glad to follow him blindly. His army soon wins a bloody revolution. Once in power, they split into factions. A vicious civil war erupts islandwide. The carnage is horrific.

After years of brutal fighting, Gokillem prevails. He declares himself the king and decrees his sons shalt rule after him. Fueled by old resentful rage, he orders the torture and murder of thousands. Their anguished cries go unheard in the night.

The tyranny endures until this regime inevitably collapses under the weight of its own corruption and insipid incompetence. Dystopian anarchy follows. Life is a merciless fight for primal survival as people perish rapidly. Paradise has become hell.

Amid the rubble, a few enlightened people dare to teach spiritual mindfulness. After long and lonely years studying old banned books in dark basements, they now surface to share forgotten truths under the long-neglected and withering tree of unity.

Sages teach that people once lived safe and free together. The secret of life is knowing the natural unity of all life. Enlightenment helps a soul live mindfully. In this way life, and society is sustainable.

Some people listen and learn. Spiritually reborn, these few brave souls elect to leave the ruins behind. They decided to find a new remote island and build a better life there. They construct wooden ships and sail away. Riding winds and currents, navigating by starlight, they voyage into a mist.

PART II

Liberty Found

Alas, we have been long led away
by ancient prejudices, and made large
sacrifices to superstition.

THOMAS PAINE

7

Resistance and Renewal

AUTHOR'S NOTE: *Any useful cautionary tale deserves a hopeful alternative ending. So, I hereby energetically take out of the law and void all dire visions in Part I. Cancel, cancel, cancel! Instead, I imagine a positive future. Pretending Candide is the storyteller, I pick up the fable at a pivot point in the Bull presidency.*

RESISTANCE TO Jason Bull's autocratic bumbling raises doubts among his supporters. The opposition party in bi-elections wins a slim majority in congress, promising all sorts of investigations.

Bull is erratic and dangerously desperate. One of the president's men, acting on conscience, leaks to the press a secret memo outlining a covert plan to bomb the Unity Tree and blame the "nature nuts." The memo reveals Bull plans a second bombing to declare martial law and impose a police state.

Outraged outcry! Hundreds and then thousands of people gather to surround the Unity Tree. "Occupy Tree Week" stretches into months. Encampments arise in every district. "Occupiers" lobby congress for Bull's impeachment and removal.

At public hearings in the House chamber, a clerk under oath testifies she'd kept copies of memos and documents that Bull had destroyed.

Evidence exposes Bull and his aides conspired with a northern district crime boss to bomb the Unity Tree. When their plot was foiled, the evidence reveals, they conspired to obstruct justice, a failed cover-up of high crimes and misdemeanors.

The House impeaches President Jason Bull. The Senate convicts him, a foregone conclusion. He's removed from office, tried for sedition and treason by a criminal jury. Found guilty, he's frog marched to prison past a crowd chanting, "Lock him up!"

Congress enacts sweeping remedial measures. Years of suppressed democratic activism pays off.

A constitutional amendment is proposed and ratified that removes all private money from public elections. Candidates and elected officials are totally banned from accepting all gifts, bribes, job offers, or favors. Penalties for corruption have teeth.

Another amendment limits the "unitary" power of the chief executive. The president still ratifies laws passed by Congress, and he still issues administrative directives to carry out those laws. But the president can't issue executive decrees the courts must enforce that are contrary to congressional laws.

In this way, the people agree that elected leaders are but trusted servants; they should not govern like kings. The rule of prevails law over the rule of leaders. People decide democracy can actually work.

Mankind [sic] being originally equals
in the order of creation, the equality could
only be destroyed by some subsequent circumstance.

THOMAS PAINE

- 8 -

Equality and Liberty

THE PACE OF CHANGE quickens across the island. Adoni Rafi and other activist women play leading roles in the Occupy movement. An ally of Adoni is Clio Devi, a descendant of Shakti and Kodesh. They engage in work to curb government abuses.

Women demand an equal voice in island affairs. The disenfranchised "Suffragettes" suffer abuses for daring to claim society must restore every woman's natural right to vote. Men in power resist mightily.

Suffrage campaigns stall within the districts and in congress until women start withholding sex. They file criminal assault and rape charges against men who refuse to accept that "no" means No!

A woman is killed. Public opinion shifts. Women win the vote. Women comprise half the electorate. Women are elected to public office at all levels of government, from local town councils to judgeships and congress. In time, a woman is elected president. Leadership transcends gender.

More social shifts occur when a famous actress, with Clio Devi and Adoni Rafi at her side, denounces sexual harassment by a lofty media mogul. The man for years abused his power to silence women. More of his victims step up to say, "Me too!"

Women expose predatory sexual misconduct by men in politics, media, the arts, the trades, business, religion, sports, and beyond. Women are believed. Time's up for male rule. Predatory men in power step down. Men feel defensive. Some retaliate.

Women in "The Reckoning" insist their bodies and wombs belong to them, not men. Women assert men never had a right to rule them. Women claim the right to be mothers only if and when they choose, not because a man or the state says they must.

Working women demand and get equal pay for equal work. They demand and get equal access to top jobs. Gender equality soon extends into equal rights for homosexual, transgender or any form of human. Within a few generations, marriage and workplace equality, under law, applies to people of all natures and abilities. The shifts take time to absorb.

Some men recognize their alpha-male bias has disadvantages. They shift their life focus from being in charge to being themselves. The men's movement gains momentum, changing men one man at a time. They gather in circles to dive deep and get real.

"New men" with raised consciousness go public about feeling liberated at releasing the ancient need to dominate women and rule the world.

Men are fed up dying younger than women from the stress and strife of male rule. Real men want to be their real selves. A new man longs to live from his heart and soul, not only his head and groin.

Gender equality trends revive love for the sacred feminine and sacred masculine in nature. A cultural awakening stirs environmental, ecological awareness and protections. Healthy lifestyles include natural foods and zero waste. Bleached reefs around the isle rebound with teeming life. Renewable clean energy becomes commonplace. A higher standard of living lifts every person above survival subsistence.

A spiritual renewal ignites in all religions. Sages and mystics, long dismissed, regain influence.

For the first time in generations, mindfulness methods of all sorts are taught to the young in school, practiced by adults in daily life. The new spirituality reinforces social equality, for all existence is light and so equally valuable. Prejudices and injustice decline into rare social blips. Becoming spiritually awakened and socially "woke" eventually becomes an everyday common courtesy, an *a priori* given fact that all life is one, so all life merits respect and love.

As librated men become the norm, wealth stops being a testament of male potency. The gap narrows between rich and poor as most people enjoy the fruit of their talent and industry. Inherited wealth loses its allure when a high quality of life is normal.

As prosperity spreads, crime declines. Criminal punishment is replaced by "restorative justice," good karma. Humane confinement becomes a last resort. Ex-offenders are integrated into civil society.

Law enforcement is still needed, so community peace officers earn honor and trust. Police are not feared like in the bad old days under Bull.

As dread of "the other" fades, military spending drops. The voluntary armed forces turn to recovery from natural disasters, like ever worsening seasons of devastating typhoons. Something is going on with the climate beyond the island. Scientists realize they need to understand global systems to know why the weather is turning dangerously unstable.

Young adults enlist for civilian national service, such as healthcare support or wetlands restoration. The military and public service veterans earn college tuition and low-interest housing loans.

Society then decides healthcare, like education, is a natural right of all, not just a privileged few. Self-reliance matters, yet a social safety net is a moral duty. People gladly vote to pay higher taxes for universal healthcare covering all. End medical debt. Social investments bless everybody. More folks are healthy, productive and living mindfully free.

In this way, island society moves closer to the spiritual values of the early settlers. The more people sense they are part of the whole, the more easily they balance freedom and responsibility. Their awakening inspires other people to behave themselves.

The nearer any government approaches to a republic
the less business there is for a king.

THOMAS PAINE

9

Reflection and Discovery

THE RESTORATION prompts people to reflect on the Bull era. They begin to seek gifts from the chaos. They "reframe" the experience, so it makes sense.

"Wasn't It Amazing?" becomes a popular party game. Players compete to put the best positive spin on the havoc Bull wrought. The game yields a curious range of discoveries.

Some of the top winners:

"Wasn't it amazing that Bull's selfish immaturity helped us mature into sensible adulthood?"

"Wasn't it amazing Bull's lawlessness compelled us to reclaim the rule of law without violence?"

"Wasn't it amazing that Bull's narcissism proved the insane absurdity of worshipping bullies?"

"Wasn't it amazing that Bull's blatant racism and sexism helped trigger racial and gender equality?"

"Wasn't it amazing that Bull, by using fear and hate to divide and conquer us, goaded us to release polarizing duality and embrace our unity?

"Wasn't it amazing that Bull's denial of island climate change, while our climate is changing, stirred our adoption of a global sensibility?"

"Wasn't it amazing that we stopped tyranny and saved democracy for posterity?"

"Wasn't it amazing that we awoke before blind nihilism destroyed us?"

A few game players, in a reaction to despair, get caught up in excessive optimism:

"Wasn't it amazing that Bull was an unwitting lightbringer who disrupted dark old institutions?"

"Wasn't it amazing that Bull was the trickster teacher who made us face our own hidden shadows, so we ascend faster into the light?"

The party game lets people imagine the best of all possible worlds, a blessing after hard times. Sadly, the game is addictive. Some gamers overdose on wild optimism, hit bottom, and enter recovery.

10

Seven Generations

RAPID CHANGES in island culture scare people. The pushback fades in each passing year. Over the next seven generations, more enlightened civil habits, like conscious commerce, become normal life. Violations of rights are rare. Most people feel safe and secure. Most people feel peaceful and creative.

A movement arises to outgrow representative democracy, which distances the government from the people. People discuss a "direct republic" where the voters elect representatives to draft bills, and then voters have the final says on all proposed laws. Direct republics can work if people educate themselves to vote intelligently, argue advocates. Voting is a natural civil right and a moral duty for all.

In self-defense, the wealthiest libercontrarians drop out of society. Citing the holy names of Jim Jolt and Pam Land, they go on strike. They expect utter financial collapse without them in control of the government (via lobbyists and puppet politicians). To their shock and terror, the island economy booms. Widespread prosperity proves the case for greater participation in democracy.

Within a few generations, direct republics govern island life. Once a year, voters get a notice of all local, district and island laws offered for their ratification. People research candidates and issues carefully, go to local and online forums. After due consideration, they vote secretly and securely on anonymous paper ballots, publicly counted, patiently, as a community celebration of democracy in action.

Ballot measures for all proposed laws offer three voting options: "Yes" or "No" or "RTA" (Revise and Try Again). Some proposed laws wind up revised repeatedly before winning passage, if they ever do. For any major policy direction shift, a supermajority of voters must consent to that big change. As a result, new laws are few yet have wide support.

As mindfulness and civility increases, so does self-reliance and decency. As the need for regulation shrinks, so does the size and reach of government. Useless laws enacted generations ago are repealed

— the conservative ideal. As equal rights and civil liberties expand, so does the quality of life for all — the progressive ideal. Greed stops being a substitute for self-worth and self-esteem.

Society stays imperfect, yet the government is generally honest and reliable. People savor freedom, harmony and prosperity in society because they savor peace and love and generosity in themselves.

One unexpected day, a masted ship of starving refugees sails into the harbor. Islanders are amazed, curious, courteous, and kind. They welcome the new arrivals, feed them, and tend to their ailments. The islanders ask the visitors to tell their story.

They'd escaped a distant land fallen into tyranny and barbarity. Drawn from all races and religions, the best and brightest of their people built a wooden ship and sailed away. Trusting wind and stars to navigate unknown seas, they chased the ghost of legendary ancestors, all enlightened, who sailed to utopia.

Their endless journey felt hopeless, they share, until land appeared on the horizon. They approached warily as the island spread out before them. Sailing into a busy commercial harbor, they expected to be boarded, questioned, or killed as invaders. Imagine their delight at the first friendly hails of greeting!

The islanders know they once were strangers in this strange land. They welcome the refugees warmly, nourish them, heal them, comfort them, ease them into island life, invite them to stay forever.

Turns out that the immigrants bring with them advanced scientific knowledge and brilliant creativity that sparks a renaissance across the island, blessing everyone in every district. In celebration, the people gather around the giant, thriving Unity Tree.

In this way, the good inhabitants of our fabled remote island evolve genuine unity and spiritual self-government. After generations of travail, by choosing democracy and natural equality, they enjoy a rebirth of freedom. Evolving practical, empathic awareness of our oneness, they restore their society and island home. Together they build their world anew.

And so the people rejoice.

A paradise once lost now is found.

About the Author

JUDAH FREED (1950–) is a seasoned journalist, author and speaker. His work won two Nautilus Book Awards and a Benjamin Franklin Book Award.

Judah studied creative writing with John Schultz and Betty Shiflett in The Story Workshop at Columbia College Chicago. He earned a double BA in communication and journalism through the University Without Walls program at Loretto Heights College (Regis). He researched communication through the Individualized MA program at Antioch.

Judah is a member of the American Society of Journalists and Authors (First Amendment, Banned Books cmtes.), PEN America, The Authors Guild, The Society of Professional Journalists, and others.

For information, JudahFreed.com

About Thomas Paine

THOMAS PAINE (1737-1809), an English-born writer and activist, is renown for his 1776 essay, *Common Sense,* a pivotal call for American independence and democracy. Paine's mind was influenced by The Enlightenment.

In his late thirties, Paine's writings, activism and scientific interests in London caught the eye of Benjamin Franklin, who in 1774 encouraged Paine to sail to Philadelphia. There Paine became the editor of *Pennsylvania Magazine.*

With rebellion in the air, Paine wrote *Common Sense,* first published January 10, 1776. Among the 2.5 million colonists, 150,000 copies sold in three months. (Paine gave his earnings to the Continental Army.) He persuaded a majority of Americans to support independence and establish the world's first modern republic. Without *Common Sense* swaying public opinion, historians concur, the revolution would have failed.

Paine next wrote the *American Crisis* series to support the grinding war effort. He began with the line, "These are the times that try men's souls."

After the war, Paine sailed to France for their revolution, voicing humanist ideals in *Rights of Man*, published in 1791, the #1 bestseller of the full 18th century in Europe and America. Aristocrats hated Paine's attack on hereditary power.

Honored at first in Franc, Paine was arrested in 1793 by the Reign of Terror for the "crime" of being English and ties to the democratic Girondin party. Imprisoned near Paris, he fell ill while John Adams' government denied his U.S. citizenship. When Robespierre fell in 1794, the new American minister to France, James Monroe, secured Paine's release. His health never recovered.

While he's a prisoner of conscience, Paine was writing *The Age of Reason*, his critique of organized religion. Published in two parts, 1794 and 1795, the book was praised in Europe, where Paine still lived. In the new United States, the book yielded a furious backlash among ardent believers.

At Jefferson's invitation, Paine sailed back to America in 1802. He was so ill that he had to be carried off the ship. Paine found himself an outcast, a casualty of the fight between John Adams and Thomas Jefferson, between the Federalists wanting an aristocracy and the democrats wanting people empowered to decide their own fates. The same battle still plays out today.

Settling in New York, Paine died seven years later in ignominy, reviled and misunderstood. One of his detractors, later repentant, dug up Paine's buried body to be entombed in England, where permission for a shrine was denied. In time, all his remains were lost except for his jawbone.

Paine's reputation finally is recovering. The U.S. Congress recently approved a memorial statue in Washington, DC. More people today know the writer' name than have read his books.

Thomas Paine changed our whole world for the better. On his great shoulders others stand.

For more information: ThomasPaine.org

The sun never shined on a cause of greater worth. 'Tis not the affair of a city, a county, a province, or a kingdom, but of a continent... [and] the habitable globe. 'Tis not the concern of a day, a year, or an age; posterity are virtually involved in the contest, and will be more or less affected, even to the end of time, by the proceedings now.

THOMAS PAINE

Appendices

COMMON SENSE;

ADDRESSED TO THE

INHABITANTS

O F

A M E R I C A,

On the following interesting

S U B J E C T S.

I. Of the Origin and Design of Government in general,
with concise Remarks on the English Constitution.

II. Of Monarchy and Hereditary Succession.

III. Thoughts on the present State of American Affairs.

IV. Of the present Ability of America, with some miscellaneous Reflections.

Man knows no Master save creating HEAVEN,
Or those whom choice and common good ordain.
THOMSON.

PHILADELPHIA;
Printed, and Sold, by R. BELL, in Third-Street.
MDCCLXXVI.

Common Sense appeared anonymously on January 10, 1776. The second edition on February 14 named him.

Paine's Original Fable

BELOW IS THE section of *Common Sense* by Thomas Paine offering the fable that I expanded into this book — given in the first seven paragraphs of Part I.

Paine voiced complex ideas in plain speech for his times. He wrote enduring truths using language ordinary people in 1776 could understand.

Readers today expect short sentences and short paragraphs. Well, 18th century writing featured long sentences in long paragraphs. Punctuation rules were different; commas marked pauses for breath.

Personal pronouns back then were always male. I tried inserting "[sic]" after all male pronouns, but it hurt readability. So, instead, please trust that if Paine was writing now, he'd modernize his pronouns.

And now we go back in time for insights today....

SOME WRITERS have so confounded society with government, as to leave little or no distinction between them; whereas they are not only different, but have different origins. Society is produced by our wants, and government by our wickedness; the former promotes our happiness positively by uniting our affections, the latter negatively by restraining our vices. The one encourages intercourse, the other creates distinctions. The first a patron, the last a punisher.

Society in every state is a blessing, but government even in its best state is but a necessary evil; in its worst state an intolerable one; for when we suffer, or are exposed to the same miseries by a government, which we might expect in a country without government, our calamity is heightened by reflecting that we furnish the means by which we suffer. Government, like dress, is the badge of lost innocence; the palaces of kings are built on the ruins of the bowers of paradise. For were the impulses of conscience clear, uniform, and irresistibly obeyed, man would need no other lawgiver; but that not being the case, he finds it necessary to surrender up a part of his property to furnish means for the protection of the rest; and this he is induced to do by the same prudence which in every other case advises him out of two evils to choose the least. Wherefore, security being the true design and end of government, it unanswerably follows, that whatever form thereof appears most likely to ensure it to us, with the least expense and greatest benefit, is preferable to all others.

In order to gain a clear and just idea of the design and end of government, let us suppose a small number of persons settled in some sequestered part of the earth, unconnected with the rest, they will then represent the first peopling of any country, or of the world. In this state of natural liberty, society will be their first thought. A thousand motives will excite them thereto, the strength of one man is so unequal to his wants, and his mind so unfitted for perpetual solitude, that he is soon obliged to seek assistance and relief of another, who in his turn requires the same. Four or five united would be able to raise a tolerable dwelling in the midst of a wilderness, but one man might labour out of the common period of life without accomplishing any thing; when he had felled his timber he could not remove it, nor erect it after it was removed; hunger in the mean time would urge him from his work, and every different want call him a different way. Disease, nay even misfortune would be death, for though neither might be mortal, yet either would disable him from living, and reduce him to a state in which he might rather be said to perish than to die.

Thus necessity, like a gravitating power, would soon form our newly arrived emigrants into society, the reciprocal blessings of which, would supersede, and render the obligations of law and government unnecessary while they remained perfectly just to each other; but as nothing but heaven is impregnable to vice, it will unavoidably happen, that in proportion as they surmount the first difficulties of emigration, which bound them together in a common cause, they will begin to relax in their duty and attachment to each other; and this remissness will point out the necessity of establishing some form of government to supply the defect of moral virtue.

Some convenient tree will afford them a State-House, under the branches of which, the whole colony may assemble to deliberate on public matters. It is more than probable that their first laws will have the title only of Regulations, and be enforced by no other penalty than public disesteem. In this first parliament every man, by natural right, will have a seat.

But as the colony increases, the public concerns will increase likewise, and the distance at which the members may be separated, will render it too inconvenient for all of them to meet on every occasion as at first, when their number was small, their habitations near, and the public concerns few and trifling. This will point out the convenience of their consenting to leave the legislative part to be managed by a select number chosen from the whole body, who are supposed to have the same concerns at stake which those who appointed them, and who will act in the same manner as the whole body would act, were they present. If the colony continues increasing, it will become necessary to augment the number of the representatives, and that the interest of every part of the colony may be attended to, it will be found best to divide the whole into convenient parts, each part sending its proper number; and that the elected might never form to themselves an interest separate from the electors, prudence will point out the propriety of having elections often; because as the elected might by that means return and mix again with the general body of the electors in a few months, their fidelity to the public will be secured by the prudent reflection of not making a rod for themselves. And as this frequent interchange will establish a common interest with every part of the community, they will mutually and naturally support each other, and on this (not on the unmeaning name of king) depends the strength of government, and the happiness of the governed.

Here then is the origin and rise of government; namely, a mode rendered necessary by the inability of moral virtue to govern the world; here too is the design and end of government, viz. freedom and security. And however our eyes may be dazzled with show, or our ears deceived by sound; however prejudice may warp our wills, or interest darken our understanding, the simple voice of nature and of reason will say, it is right.

Perhaps the sentiments contained in [these] pages,
are not yet sufficiently fashionable to procure them
general favour; a long habit of not thinking a thing
wrong, gives it a superficial appearance of being right,
and raises at first a formidable outcry in defense
of custom. But the tumult soon subsides.
Time makes more converts than reason.

THOMAS PAINE

Read the companion book

MAKING GL🌐BAL SENSE

Grounded HOPE for democracy and the earth inspired by Thomas Paine's COMMON SENSE

Why One Billion of Us Build Our World Anew

IN HARD TIMES of climate change
when autocracies outnumber democracies,
a global sense of our natural oneness grounds us,
so we unite to create a free and sustainable future.

———————— 〰 ————————

"Judah Freed has taken the gauntlet from Thomas Paine
and other innovators of democracy to guide us toward
the evolution of democracy itself. *Making Global Sense*
is a vital and wonderful book, well written and inspired."

– **Barbara Marx Hubbard**, *Conscious Evolution (she saw draft)*

———————— 〰 ————————

A journey for these times that try our souls

Text is set in Utopia, an Adobe Originals typeface designed by Robert Slimbach in 1989, based on such 18th century Transitional fonts as Baskerville.

Headlines are set in Adobe Myriad Pro, a Humanist sans-serif font designed by Robert Slimbach and Carol Twombly with Christopher Slye and Fred Brady, released in 1992.

The title and versa page quotes are set in Caslon Antique, designed in 1894 by Berne Nadall to emulate the chipped look of worn metal type. Based on Dutch baroque typefaces, Caslon was created in 1722 by the London typographer William Caslon. Popular among 18th century printers, Caslon was used to print *Common Sense* and The Declaration of Independence.